Boston ivy

Little leaf linden

Japanese cherry

Pin oak

Silver maple

Common sassafras

Norway maple

Japanese elm

Callery pear

American linden

Quaking aspen

Northern red oak

Red maple

American elm

for all the daydreamers

Random House Studio with colophon is a trademark of Penguin Random House LLC.

Visit us on the Web! rhcbooks.com

Educators and librarians, for a variety of teaching tools, visit us at RHTeachersLibrarians.com

Library of Congress Cataloging-in-Publication Data

Names: Sicuro, Aimée, author. Title: If you find a leaf / Aimée Sicuro. Description: First edition. | New York : Random House Studio, [2022] | Audience: Ages 4–8. | Summary: "A young artist draws inspiration from the leaves she collects and every leaf sparks a new idea"—Provided by publisher. Identifiers: LCCN 2021042518 (print) | LCCN 2021042519 (ebook) | ISBN 978-0-593-30659-8 (trade) | ISBN 978-0-593-30660-4 (lib. bdg.) | ISBN 978-0-593-30661-1 (ebook) Subjects: CYAC: Stories in rhyme. | Leaves—Fiction. | Imagination—Fiction. | LCGFT: Picture books. | Stories in rhyme. Classification: LCC PZ8.3.S5713 If 2022 (print) | LCC PZ8.3.S5713 (ebook) | DDC [E]—dc23

The artist used ink, watercolor, charcoal, photography, and collage to create the illustrations for this book. The text of this book is set in 19-point Bell MT Pro Semibold. Interior design by Rachael Cole

MANUFACTURED IN CHINA
10 9 8 7 6 5 4 3 2 1
First Edition

IF YOU FIND a leaf

aimée sicuro

RANDOM HOUSE STUDIO ⌂ NEW YORK

If you find a leaf

You could dream the day away.

It could be a hat on a chilly day.

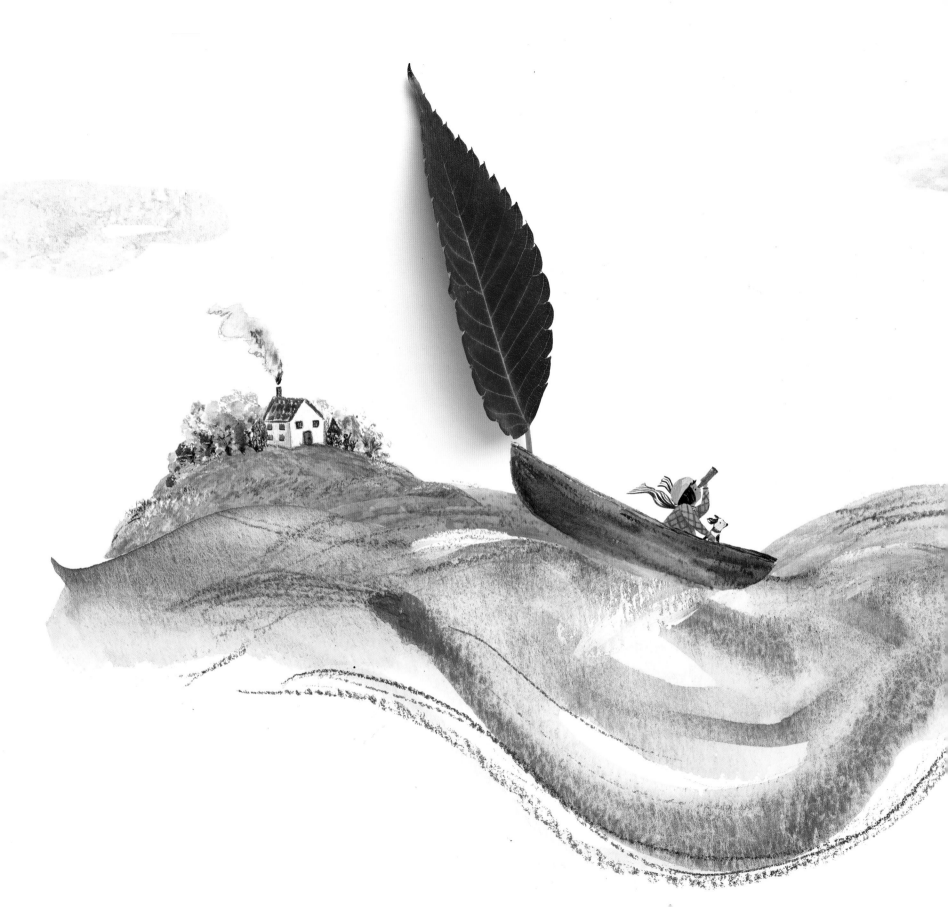

Or a boat so you could sail far, far away.

You could float high above the trees.

Parachuting down to see all the other leaves.

If you find a leaf, it could be a hammock.

A place for you to rest and sway in a gentle breeze.

It could be your Halloween disguise.

A funny mask with cut-out spooky eyes.

A leafy crown,

a dancer's skirt,

or a superhero's cape.

It could be anything you wish to make.

If you find a leaf, it could be your muse.

Hanging high for you to paint its changing hues.

You could go apple picking and pumpkin picking too.

Zooming up the road with your leafy crew.

It could be a horn that blows, announcing that we're here.

A leafy parade to celebrate our favorite time of year.

If you find a leaf, it could be a glowing
fire to gather round and sing with friends.

Or a comfy blanket for you to snuggle in.

And when the days grow shorter and the last leaf falls,
I know it's time to say goodbye. Winter calls.

Until the spring, when all is green
and leafy shoots open toward the sun.

When I first started making artwork for this book, I photographed the illustrated scenes. Noticing that my leaves quickly lost their vibrant color and became brittle, I experimented with different techniques to preserve them. I tried glycerin baths, leaf-pressing methods, wax dipping, acrylic spray, and Mod Podge. These experiments all worked and affected the leaves in different ways. The glycerin bath technique was my favorite because it left the leaves soft and flexible.

Here is how to use the glycerin bath method. You may need a grown-up's help for some of the steps.

You will need two plastic containers that can stack together, glycerin (commonly found in the drugstore or online), and water.

1. Collect fall leaves in a variety of colors, shapes, and sizes. Try to find leaves that have recently fallen and don't feel too dry or brittle.

2. Mix one part glycerin and two parts water in one of the plastic containers.

3. Submerge your fresh fall leaves in the mixture, making sure the leaves are separate and not overlapping.

4. Stack the remaining container on top of the leaves in the solution in the other container as a weight to ensure the leaves remain covered.
5. Leave in the solution for three to five days.
6. Remove your leaves from the solution and gently pat them dry with paper towels. Your leaves will be soft and pliable, with the fall colors beautifully preserved and easy to work with.

Maybe it's a hat.

Or an umbrella.

Now that you have your preserved leaves, you're ready to create your own leafy world. Lay your leaf on a piece of paper and look carefully at the shape. What do you see? Flip the leaf in all different directions until the leaf shape sparks your imagination. Use a pencil to complete your idea, and if you'd like, color in your drawing with whatever supplies you have on hand. Use glue or Mod Podge to stick your leaf in place. Have fun creating!

Could your leaf be a kite?

Sugar maple

Honey locust

Northern red oak

Japanese maple

Armenian plum

Silver maple

Japanese elm

Ginkgo biloba

Callery pear

Quaking aspen

Red maple

American basswood

Ginkgo biloba

Flowering dogwood

Norway maple